Janine,
With best wishes,

Berry

8.10.09

MORTIMER – THE GREAT ESCAPE

MORTIMER –
THE GREAT ESCAPE

Barry Rochfort

Book Guild Publishing
Sussex, England

First published in Great Britain in 2006 by
The Book Guild Ltd,
25 High Street,
Lewes, East Sussex
BN7 2LU

Typesetting in Souvenir Light by
IML Typographers, Birkenhead, Merseyside

Printed in Great Britain by
CPI Bath

A catalogue record for this book is
available from The British Library

ISBN 1 84624 033 6

Contents

Chapter 1

In the Beginning

It was a stormy night when Mortimer, the marmot, slipped out of his burrow at London Zoo and headed for the fence. Lightning flashed everywhere like sparklers on Bonfire Night and thunder crashed loudly round the city, while the rain fell like a waterfall to make puddles and mud. When Mortimer reached the fence, he was wet through and cold. He pressed his nose hard against the wire to see what was outside his prison.

A light flashed near by. A dog growled menacingly. Shivers of fright and excitement rippled up and down Mortimer's spine, even though he was desperate to escape and start his long journey. He closed his eyes to dream up some braveness. But in his imagination, the only picture he could see was of his mother and father and his brothers and sisters standing at the entrance to his burrow crying and shaking their heads in sorrow.

'Where has my darling Mortimer gone?' he imagined his mother crying. 'I'll never see him again.'

'Of course you will,' his father seemed to comfort

her, 'he's probably around somewhere. You know how he loves to play hide and seek and other sorts of tricks.'

'Yes, I know, Otto,' his mother would probably be saying, 'but he's been gone for over two days and the weather has been awful. I'm afraid he's lost. Perhaps he's been caught and killed by one of the guard dogs.'

Banishing these thoughts from his mind, Mortimer took a deep breath and instead tried to imagine he was an intrepid explorer heading out into the unknown. Because he was worried about losing the courage he pretended he had, he scurried off to the escape tunnel he had been digging. After all, this was a mind-boggling adventure he was about to start, and even humans would find it difficult. Anyway, at his escape tunnel he hoped to become really brave again and make his great escape. He dropped into the first chamber and for a moment started thinking about what was going on and what had happened to bring him there. What was he doing? He was trying to escape from human captivity, even though he was very fond of them and also loved his marmot family dearly. But the real start of his journey had begun some years ago in the Austrian Alps where his parents had grown up in the mountains. So what happened? This story tells you; please read on:

Otto, Mortimer's father, was an alpine marmot who used to live in the great mountains in the Tyrol part of Austria. Marmots are the biggest members of the squirrel family. A marmot is larger than a rabbit, has thicker fur and a shorter tail. Marmots burrow underground and make large nesting chambers, which are connected sometimes by very, very long tunnels. They can be shy creatures. Unlike many other members of his family, Otto was highly intelligent and had some magical gifts even he did not know about – yet.

One morning in early springtime with the sun trying to warm itself up, Otto came out of his burrow for a good, long stretch after his long winter sleep. His world was a wonderful world of fir trees, wild flowers and waterfalls, of high-flying birds and buzzing bees, and of any other magic thing you would ever want to think about. He gazed around and whistled a happy tune.

'I'm off to play on the glacier,' Otto announced to his family. 'Anyone coming along?'

'No,' shouted his brothers and sisters.

'Oh, come on,' Otto pleaded. 'Let's have a race and see who can slide down the glacier fastest.'

'NO,' was the answer. 'Away you go,' scowled Brunhilda, his eldest sister, who was having a bit of a scrap with her youngest brother who was trying to pull her tail.

'Whoopie!' shouted Otto to anyone who might be listening. 'What a wheeze,' he called out joyously as he pushed off down the hill and quickly found himself hurtling out of control on his bottom down the famous Hoch Gletcher glacier in the valley below the Grossglockner alp.

'Vorsicht,' someone shouted. 'Look out!'

Too late! Otto thumped into a huge boulder and tumbled over and over and over before finishing up on a huge pile of soft, pale green moss. He had whacked

3

his head on something very hard, saw a sky full of stars and then realised he now had a nasty pain in his head.

'What's going on?' demanded a plump mother marmot as she came out of her burrow nearby. 'Silly boy,' she scolded when she saw Otto. 'You should have known better than to go out on the glacier today, it's far too slippery.' Then she called to her daughter, Birgitte, 'Come and help me get this silly boy into the kitchen. He's hurt his head.' This was easier said than done because Otto was a large marmot. They pulled and pulled and gradually dragged him into their kitchen where they all collapsed in a heap.

'Oh dear,' chuckled mother marmot, 'how silly of us to fall down too.' Otto had to stifle a chuckle because he really could have got up and waddled in if they had let him. So instead he made some painful sounding groans just to make them feel that he really had hurt himself, especially as they had been so kind and careful, and he didn't want to disappoint.

'Thank you,' he said very politely. 'My tail got caught up with my back feet and I couldn't use them as brakes or my tail as a rudder.' They all laughed.

The kitchen was big and warm, and smelled fresh and sweet. Herbs and grasses were set out on the back wall to dry. The table was heavy laden with the midday meal spread out on the crisp blue and white tablecloth. Mother marmot inspected Otto and noticed that he had a nasty gash on the side of his head, which Birgitte bandaged up expertly.

'Who are you?' she asked curiously.

'Yes, who are you and where do you come from?' mother marmot also asked.

5

'I'm, mmmm Ot Ot Otto from the Hoch Gletcher,' he stammered, for he was still a little shocked from his fall. 'I, I, I was just out for a bit of fun and ... well, here I am,' he sighed. 'Just as well my brothers and sisters refused to come out on the glacier today or you would have had a whole burrowful of wounded marmots!'

And so started a rather special friendship. Otto had now met the Stille family and their very pretty daughter Birgitte. Otto thought that she was the prettiest girl marmot he would ever see. Birgitte and Otto fell in love at first sight and determined to get married and live happily together ever after.

The marriage was soon arranged. It was a big wedding. All the uncles and aunts and cousins were there, and lots and lots of friends. In fact, nearly every marmot in their part of the mountains was there. Everyone had terrific fun and there was lots of dancing and merrymaking and feasting on nuts, berries and grass seeds. Because everyone was so happy they all jumped onto the glacier and slid to the bottom, where they said goodbye to Otto and Birgitte as they set off down the valley for their honeymoon.

'Goodbye!' everyone shouted. '*Auf wiedersehen! Good luck!*'

'Goodbye,' Otto and Birgitte called back as they scampered along their way far down the mountain towards the town of Lienz, a place Otto had heard about and wanted to visit. Quite how he came to know about it was a mystery to him just now. They were both so happy and quite unaware of what was about to happen to them.

Chapter 2

Capture

Quite a long way down the mountain, holding Birgitte's hand, Otto guided her quietly along the top ledge of a balcony belonging to what he realised was a rather nice hotel on the outskirts of Lienz. They crept their way along cautiously, hidden by some large plants, and stopped suddenly. Otto whispered to Birgitte to be quiet. There was silence, but only for a moment. Otto had spotted some humans. He had seen such creatures before, high up in the mountain, but never close enough to hear them talk.

A man with a big beard in the group said, 'We must take care of the alpine area. It is very special.'

Otto nearly fell over with astonishment as the man spoke. It was really quite extraordinary – Otto could understand what the human was saying. He could understand human language even though it was very different from the way marmots communicated. For a moment he felt very frightened, especially when the man carried on talking, saying, 'The mountains are precious and the birds are wonderful, but the trees seem to be suffering from polluted rain. What worries me most of all is that some of the small animals and plants are becoming fewer and fewer. Even the marmots are under threat.'

'We need to capture some of them for a conservation programme,' said another man. Otto was intrigued and whispered to Birgitte, who until then had not been sure what was going on. She was absolutely amazed as she realised she, too, could understand human speech.

'I want to collect some marmots and take them back to London Zoo,' said the man with the beard. 'I have already made a marvellous alpine garden area outside my office where we could breed them and study them and preserve their long-term future.'

Otto did not understand what 'collect' and 'London Zoo' meant. For a moment he quite forgot himself and imagined that the humans were just another kind of marmot. If he could understand what the humans were saying, then he was sure the humans could jolly well understand what he was saying. So, bold as brass, taking Birgitte by the hand, Otto jumped onto the balcony floor and waddled across to ask the humans what was going on.

Before you could say 'yum, jelly beans' the humans had pounced on Otto and Birgitte, grabbing them firmly. Whistling with fury (for that is what marmots can do) Birgitte and Otto sank their teeth into the bearded man's hand. The next thing Otto knew was that after flying through the air he hit his head and ... stars were all he could see – once again!

Birgitte was terrified but kept very still so that the humans might think she was dead. She was very much

alive and alert to any escape she could make. One man, who turned out to be a vet, said he thought she was in shock but otherwise she was all right. He examined Otto and bandaged him up while he was still unconscious. Just as well, because Otto would have had another bite given the chance.

When he came to, Otto found a very angry but worried Birgitte cuddling up to him. They were in a cage. 'We must escape!' he said, and immediately started to look around. Birgitte agreed.

'I'm so sorry, Birgitte, but there seems to be no way out.' He stroked her head and patted her back. Then, in a fit of fury he strode to the edge of the cage and roared at the top of his voice, 'LET US OUT OF HERE AT ONCE, IF NOT FASTER!!'

Who on earth did Otto think he was that humans would either understand him or obey his command? Soon the humans brought them some bedding of pine needles and moss, some food and water. Even though the humans spoke softly and kindly to them, Otto and Birgitte were very suspicious about whether the humans might want to harm them.

'Turn disaster into something positive,' said Otto philosophically. 'We must just sit back and see how things develop. It could be very interesting. Very interesting indeed.'

However, in his thoughts, Otto wondered what the humans really meant to do with them. He was absolutely amazed that he could understand the humans' language. After all, this was all so new to him, but suddenly it became very clear that their freedom to roam the mountains seemed lost forever.

They were to be taken away, far away to a strange land.

There was silence and brooding in their cage.

Chapter 3

Behind Bars

Lights appeared from nowhere and the man with the beard mumbled something to Otto and Birgitte, which they could not understand. Then he fed them with some very tasty nuts in a red dish alongside a bowl of water. Otto was sure he could still understand humans even if he did not catch what the bearded man was saying or really know what was going on. Strange journeying now began, mostly in the dark. Every now and then their cage would stop wobbling about and there would be silence, followed by some banging and crashing. Each time this happened the same routine would take place – noise, lights, talk, food, darkness – and they would start moving again. This carried on happening for a very long time until one stop, which Birgitte thought was a bit different. It was a terribly bumpy stop and she complained to Otto. They listened intently to every noise they could hear.

'Right,' said the bearded man to Otto and Birgitte, 'Next stop London Zoo.' With that the lights went out, the door banged and they started moving again.

'What's a zoo?' asked Birgitte worriedly.

'A zoo? I don't know. It's an odd word,' replied Otto as he rolled it about his tongue. He was soon convinced he did not like the word 'zoo' at all; to him it meant unhappiness but he was not sure why.

A long while later all movement stopped. There was complete silence. Then some muffled voices could be heard. The doors opened and flashing lights dazzled Otto and Birgitte as their cage was taken out, swung around, and then banged down on the ground. Otto was half blinded by the light but could see enough to tell that the cage door had sprung open.

'Quickly,' he yelled at Birgitte. 'We can escape. This way,' he shouted as he tore off into the dark. They scuttled away, looking for somewhere to hide. The feeling of freedom was terrific. The humans were shouting and lights flashed everywhere. Otto and Birgitte managed to dart between the torch beams.

'Where are they?' someone shouted at the top of his voice.

'Leave them,' replied the voice of the man with the beard. 'They'll be all right. It's late. We'll look for them in the morning.'

Otto stopped dead in his tracks. He pulled Birgitte close to his side. 'Shhhh,' he whispered. There was silence. Why had they been left alone in the dark, wondered Otto. Birgitte was still looking around. Suddenly, the truth dawned on Otto.

'Oh, no,' he cried. 'They have put us into a very big cage.' Birgitte stamped her foot on the ground and they both whistled in anger before they hugged each other and decided to wait until dawn before trying to do anything else. At least they had each other to talk

13

to because the noises where they sat were so loud and unpleasant they could not sleep. As the first light of day came they could see enough to start exploring where they were.

'It does look like a nice big cage with all sorts of interesting countryside,' said Otto as they tiptoed about.

'Look! A burrow. Let's hide here,' said Birgitte.

They scuttled inside and came to a chamber. The floor was very hard and there was some funny-looking soft material lying around. They liked it, and as they were very tired, lay down, and soon fell asleep. Later, much later, after they had woken up, Otto went exploring out of the burrow. In the broad daylight, the sun was shining. Their new cage was enormous, with high fencing which looked like a whole lot of holes held together by wire all around it to prevent escape. It was next to the zookeeper's house. The ground was rocky and some fir trees grew there, together with lots of pretty alpine flowers. It also had large granite slabs and a small stream, which came from a spring by the fence and flowed over some rocks into a pond. Otto gathered some food and went back to the burrow entrance where Birgitte was watching out for him. If there had been any danger she would have given a whistle for him to scurry back.

'I'm afraid,' he said to Birgitte, 'we are trapped. There seems to be no escape.'

'I was afraid of that,' Birgitte replied sadly, 'we will just have to accept our situation,' she said bravely. A little tear came to her eye as she thought of her home and family. She missed them terribly.

14

15

And so, Otto and Birgitte had to settle down to married life within the confines of London Zoo. Otto, ever the optimist and determined to make the best of things, struck up a good friendship with the bearded man. Birgitte was not too fond of him because of what he had done to them even though she did not like harbouring a grudge. Consequently, although she could understand what the bearded man was saying, she never let on to him. Anyway, she could get whatever information she wanted from Otto if she wasn't about during one of their chats.

Mr Beard, as Otto now called him, was a keen radio fan and always seemed to be listening to London Radio or BBC Radio Three or Radio Four. Otto liked listening to the radio and he learnt many things as he lay basking in the sun near Mr Beard's front door.

By now, Mr Beard was beginning to realise that Otto could understand him and was therefore a most amazing creature. He did not, however, appreciate that Birgitte could understand him too. He would talk to Otto for hours about all sorts of things. As a result of these curious 'conversations' Otto became a very learned marmot. He learned, for instance, that London was the capital city of the United Kingdom. It was a very long way from his home country of Austria. All this information he passed on to Birgitte, who found it fascinating. London Zoo, they understood, was very important because it not only collected all sorts of different creatures from all over the world for humans to see and study, but it also helped prevent many animals from becoming extinct.

'Conservation is what it's called,' Mr Beard used to

say ponderously. 'Yes, looking after animals here is called conservation.'

'Mmmm,' mumbled Otto in his thoughtful way to this sort of remark.

'Yes,' said Mr Beard on the first occasion, ' and you two are the first British alpine marmots.'

'My goodness me,' Otto said. 'The start of a new family. From now on I will not be known as Herr Otto Hoch Gletcher but as Mr Otto High-Glacier. I will celebrate my new nationality!'

Mr Beard was most amused as 'high glacier' was the direct translation of 'hoch gletcher'. However, despite Otto and Birgitte being declared British, Birgitte very firmly decided to keep her name as it was; Bridget, the English version, did not sound right to her.

'What a good idea,' said Mr Beard. 'I understand and approve. I am very proud of you,' he added pompously. He had good reason to be proud because these two marmots were now famous and could be seen on television. London Zoo was suddenly making a lot more money because so many people were coming to see the marmots, and toy marmots were fast becoming as popular as teddy bears with children.

Much of the fame they now had went to Otto's head and he felt he ought to have someone to carry on the family name. He thought it would be very nice to have a large family to join in the fun he and Birgitte were having. Before long Birgitte announced she was expecting her firstborn. Otto was 'EGGSTATIC' and rushed off to tell Mr Beard.

17

'Mr Beard, Mr Beard,' Otto shrieked excitedly, 'Birgitte is going to have a baby!'

Mr Beard was so delighted and so proud about this that anyone would think *he* was to be the father. An announcement was made in the newspapers, on television and on the radio. Everyone was excited. The number of zoo visitors rose even further. However, things were not to go smoothly because after supper one evening, Birgitte suddenly fell ill with a tummy upset of some kind.

'I do feel terribly sick,' whimpered Birgitte, 'it must have been something I ate. Oh dear, I feel all hot and sweaty. I feel dreadful. Oh, Otto, I feel as if I could die!'

'Oh, dread,' whimpered Otto as he cradled Birgitte in his arms. 'I do love you,' he whispered tenderly. 'Don't die. Please try hard to live.'

Birgitte tried to smile, but her eyes closed and she fell limp.

Chapter 4

Commotion in the Burrow

Mr Beard was very worried about Birgitte's bad cough, sore throat and chest. It sounded like a nasty flu bug, which affects humans. Otto had told him the bad news but had disappeared before the vet could be called, and had not been seen since. Birgitte was very ill indeed and Otto did his best to nurse her. He would sneak out at night to collect food, a little of which Birgitte would eat as she snuggled in the nest Otto had made for her.

All seemed far from well. Storms raged outside the burrow and water was trickling down from the entrance and wetting part of the floor. Birgitte seemed to be getting worse. One morning, as Otto was trying to stop the water from reaching the bedding, Birgitte called out to him. Otto rushed to her side. Suddenly there was a tiny, little squeak from a new-born marmot. Birgitte smiled and laughed with joy.

'Is it a boy or a girl?' she asked. Otto was confused for a moment. He thought his wife was desperately ill.

'Er, let me see,' he muttered. 'Yes, yes, yes,' he

19

shouted. 'You're not sick after all. Oh, you clever girl, you clever girl – it's a boy!'

'Thank you,' whispered Birgitte in terrific excitement, her face radiating happiness. 'What shall we call him?'

'Mortimer!' said Otto most emphatically, as he looked at his cooing wife and gurgling son. Otto was so proud of them both and so happy.

Above ground Mr Beard was getting ready to dig up the burrow, convinced that the marmots were dead. It was a week since he had seen any sign of them, though he had noticed that the food he put out had been taken. He was cross with himself for not having put in a glass observation window when the burrow was being built so that the marmots could be observed in their nest.

Apart from night-time forays by Otto to collect food, the family stayed firmly underground until Mortimer was a week old and Birgitte felt ready to take him out to meet Mr Beard. When they did come out it was into a black night, which was wet and blowing a gale. There was no one about; not a soul. Oh, what a disappointment for them; clearly their time clocks were quite wonky.

'Don't worry,' said Otto. 'I'll knock on Mr Beard's window.' And he did, and he did, and he did. A curtain twitched, and then twitched again. A light came on, the curtains parted, the window opened and a bleary Mr Beard looked out.

'Otto, it's the middle of the night. Why are you waking me up so early?' he asked sleepily, quite forgetting for a moment that he had not seen either

Otto or Birgitte for a whole week. 'I was at a Royal Society lecture last night and did not come home until late after a very big meal and far too much wine to drink. My head is sore. Gosh,' he exclaimed, 'it's you! I haven't seen you for some time. What's going on? Where have you been?' he suddenly asked sternly.

'Mr Beard,' said Otto, a little warily but drawing himself up to his full height, 'Birgitte and I wish to introduce our baby.'

Oh wow! That caused a flurry of excited activity by Mr Beard, whose headache disappeared immediately. He jumped out of bed, put on his dressing gown and slippers and rushed round to the marmot pen.

'A baby marmot,' Otto told him, a trifle gruffly.

'I know, I know that,' said Mr Beard. 'Is it a boy or a girl? That's what I want to know.'

'A boy,' said Birgitte, who could speak English fairly well now, but with quite a pronounced accent and couldn't resist speaking to Mr Beard for the first time. Mr Beard danced around with terrific excitement – this was great news.

'We are calling him Mortimer,' said Otto proudly.

'Mortimer, Mortimer?' said Mr Beard calming himself down by asking a kind of question. 'Interesting,' he said seriously for a moment. 'Interesting. The boy should go far with a name like that. I thought you might have called him Oscar or something suitably Austrian.'

'No, no,' said Otto, 'he is the first of the true British-born marmots so he should have a nice English name.'

21

Mr Beard felt very proud, and so did Otto and Birgitte even though they were all soaking wet by now. Mortimer burped loudly, his parents mumbled apologies and said they must take him inside or he would catch his death of cold. Little did they realise what was in store for their baby when he grew up.

Chapter 5

Mortimer Determines to Discover His Identity

As he was growing up, Mortimer determined to make sure everyone knew he was an adventurous marmot. By now he had several brothers and sisters who were born at regular intervals. It seemed that no sooner had he managed to get some free time away from them all to do his own thing when there would be some more little ones to help look after. Always getting into close scrapes, he could be very annoying to his brothers and sisters when he tried to get them to join in his fantasy games. By the time he was a young 'teenager' though, Mortimer was less keen on doing what he was asked because he wanted to make his own decisions.

Mortimer would explore the marmot enclosure, which had been greatly increased in size to house other marmot families brought in from Austria as part of Mr Beard's conservation programme. There were even some which Mortimer believed came from the French Alps.

'What a strange lot,' he said of these newcomers as

24

he sat outside his burrow under the shade of a fir tree. 'They seem to be so shy and always look down when anyone speaks to them. They are far too respectful – even to me!' he opined. 'I really do get bored with them. They are very dull and seem to have no enthusiasm for life. They carry their tails low, speak quietly and never, never answer back. What's got into them?' he asked himself.

One day, bent on mischief, he spotted the other marmots all huddling round something, so he pottered over for a look. It seemed they were discussing whether to eat the nuts from a strange-looking fir cone. None of them seemed able to make a decision. Mortimer could not resist action.

'Watch out,' he shouted as he rushed in, sweeping the other marmots aside, grabbing the fir cone and sprinting off with it. 'You're all boring, BORING, B-O-R-I-N-G,' he yelled rudely as he tapped the nuts out of the cone onto a stone. Then, in an act of absolute defiance, he threw the empty cone back at the others and disappeared into his burrow.

Because of such bad manners, Mortimer was not popular in marmot land, and everyone ignored him. This state of affairs suited him well because it let him explore all of marmot land alone. Quite soon his adventures became uninteresting and he was seriously worried that life was not meant to be like this for a marmot like him. He wanted to explore further. However, without getting out of the big cage he could not explore the rest of the zoo, let alone anywhere else.

'Mmmmmm,' he thought out loud to himself. 'I

must get out of here. But how? If I ask Mr Beard he might become suspicious and say "no". I must have a cunning plan. A cunning plan will get me out of here without anyone knowing.' Then, speaking sternly to himself, he said, 'I must escape. I must find out who I am and where I really belong. Anyway, an adventure or two would be fun. Ooooh,' he giggled, 'I feel excitement welling up inside me. It's a wonderful tingly feeling.'

Mortimer rushed out of his burrow and tore around outside till he was so exhausted he could only just jump up onto a rock by the water pool. As he did so he slipped and nearly fell in.

'Behave yourself,' he said to himself. Then, pretending to look frightfully important, he resolved, 'I will behave myself properly while I think out my plans. I will decide what to do. I will be a model young marmot. I shall be polite and very well-mannered. Then, when I am ready,' he whispered to himself and rubbed his hands with glee, 'and when no one is in the least suspicious, I will strike!' He punched the air and fell off the rock and into the pool. He rolled about and then sat there laughing for a moment. Then, as he clambered out of the water, said to himself, 'Quietly, I will slip away in the night and escape. All the best adventures start by slipping away in the night. *And* there should be a full moon for good luck!'

Mortimer felt nothing but excitement and rushed off to his burrow to start his preparations and draw up his plans.

Chapter 6

Adventurous Plans

The radio in Mr Beard's house blared out of the window some boring talk about the army and war. It was so loud Mortimer could not shut it out of his mind. Then he had to laugh as some pompous general started speaking: 'War is not what I am interested in. It is battle that interests me. Planning for battle,' the general harrumphed, 'planning for battle is the most important thing. You must have a clear and simple objective. Then you can work out how best to achieve it!' The general sounded triumphant.

'What does the old codger mean, exactly?' Mortimer asked himself, suddenly taking note of what was being said on the radio. He scuttled off to his burrow and looked up the word 'objective' in his dictionary. It said something like: military thing to do, to achieve.

'Well, I'm not really interested in army things,' Mortimer thought, 'but I do suppose the word "objective" might be useful. I shall think about it.' And he did, for a whole afternoon as he lay out on a rock sunning himself.

'Mmmm, objective, objective; what is my objective?' Then it dawned on him. 'Yes, of course, what I really want to do is to visit the place where my parents were born in faraway Austria. There I could meet my relatives and discover my roots.'

This, of course, was all very well. What Mortimer had not appreciated was the size of the task. He would have to get to Austria and find his way to the Hoch Gletcher in the shadow of the Grossglockner, which was the highest alp in Austria. He knew that from his geography lessons at his marmot school. He would have to cross the English Channel and travel across France and Germany and into Austria, a very long journey of many hundreds of miles.

'Could I really walk there?' he wondered. 'Don't be silly,' he muttered angrily to himself. 'Of course not. It would probably take me all of my life even if I scampered along at my fastest.' He was disappointed at this but decided that the venture would need lots of thought and research. He was going to do it, even if it killed him – which it might. He determined there and then to find out where it was he had to go and how to get there. He would listen to the radio, read travel books and brochures, and ask Mr Beard questions. Birgitte had taught Mortimer to read at an early age. He loved books because he could learn so much from them. With a book he could never be bored, and the more he read as a youngster the better his young brain would remember things. After all, our brains are at their most retentive when we are young.

And so, one day Mortimer sidled up to Mr Beard's window to try him out with a question. 'Mr Beard,' he said, 'I want to do some geographical research about Europe and pretend I am planning a visit to Austria. I shall need some maps, travel books and so on,' he said, trying to be as casual as possible.

'Oh, yes?' replied Mr Beard slowly, looking most suspiciously at Mortimer. 'Some maps and travel books, eh? From the look in your eye and the quiver in your voice and your shuffling about, I get the impression that you are not telling me the truth. I suspect you are planning to escape!'

Mortimer felt a dull and unhappy feeling in his tummy. How on earth could Mr Beard have guessed his plans so soon? This was a disastrous state of affairs. 'Nnnnn, no,' he stuttered. 'I, I, I ...' He could not get the words out. If marmots could blush, Mortimer would have been fire-engine red!

'Oh, all right,' muttered Mr Beard. 'Why not indeed? I'd want to escape if I were you. However, I am not. Not only that, but escape from London Zoo is impossible. So why shouldn't you pretend? It will be a good exercise in your geography lessons. I will get you some maps, travel books and brochures. Plan your escape and tell me how you would get to Austria.' With that he shut the window, leaving an amazed and confused Mortimer not quite sure of what was going on.

Later that day when Mortimer had come out of his burrow after a snooze, he found a bundle of books and papers put there by Mr Beard. As it was a nice summer day he dragged them over to some nearby grass and set to work. He raced through a very interesting book on Austria by someone called Fodor.

Soon Mortimer was imagining he was in the mountains. In his mind it was late summer and the days were deep blue and clear, and the tree crests were outlined in the crystal air. Yellow fungus gleamed, each like a tiny lantern, in the dark shade of the forest; the bilberries were ripe, plump and ready to eat. Lichen was on every tree trunk and branch, fresh green and frilly in the clean mountain air. Everything was tinted with the deepest, clearest colours. There was a cool darkness in the shadows. The birch tree trunks were all white and silvery, and swallows still circled about in the clear blue sky. Often, afternoon brought enormous clouds and the threat of storms, and rotten apples would plump onto rain-fresh grass, flattened by sudden wind-gusts. Such were Mortimer's imaginings.

'How go the plans?' asked Mr Beard.

'Oh, oh,' spluttered Mortimer who had not noticed Mr Beard approach.

'Here, let me spread the map out,' said Mr Beard as he unfolded a huge map of Europe. The wind ruffled it so Mr Beard placed a stone at each corner to hold it down. 'There you are. Now you can have a good look,' said Mr Beard as he stood up to leave.

'Thank you,' muttered Mortimer politely as he reached for his pencil and notebook. First, he located London and then followed the red lines to Dover.

'So that's where the English Channel starts,' he talked out loud. He made notes as far as Calais in France. Then the route became complicated. However, he did find the Grossglockner on the map. In the back of his mind he remembered a map-reading trick learnt during a geography lesson. He ducked into his burrow workshop and collected some BluTack and string.

'The shortest distance between two points is a straight line,' he muttered. 'So, we stick one end of the string on Calais and put the other end on the Gross Glockner alp.' He did this only to find the string was too short and had pulled off the Calais mark. 'Silly me,' he said and fetched some more string.

After a while, he managed to set things out properly. He wandered up and down the string several times before deciding that the best route was from Calais via Rheims and Metz in France, and then to Saarbrucken, Stuttgart and Munich in Germany before crossing into Austria. 'From there,' he was talking out loud now, 'I find my way to Kitzbuhel, up Pass Thurn to Mittersil and then turn south and up the Hochalpenstrasse to Grandfather's house! Easy peasy,' he said, knowing perfectly well that it would not be.

He marched up and down that piece of string on the map until he knew the route inside out and back to front. All the while he was trying to work out how he was going to get there. He knew about lorries, cars and trains. On the radio he frequently heard reports about imports and exports and lorries and cars travelling to Europe, and felt he could do the same. After all, it did seem logical.

'I shall have to thumb lifts,' he told himself. Hitch-hiking was the cheapest form of travel. 'But will anyone see me?' Judging by the number of little animals he had heard about being killed on the roads, he thought that 'thumbing a lift' would be distinctly dangerous, not to say out of the question, really. He decided to resort to his usual good manners and ask politely.

He was itching to go and busied himself over his plans. He would fatten himself up before escaping and would then rely on friendly drivers to feed him on the way should he not find any food himself.

A few days later Mr Beard was looking for Mortimer and bumped into Otto.

'Otto, have you seen Mortimer recently?' asked Mr Beard.

'No, I haven't, come to think of it. He's not in his burrow,' replied Otto, somewhat concerned.

'So,' snarled Mr Beard, 'the young rascal has disappeared after all.'

'What do you mean?' Otto enquired.

'Oh, never mind,' said Mr Beard somewhat angrily, and returned to his office.

Mortimer, as part of his plans, had taken to disappearing for a few days at a time. He pretended to everybody that he was studying and wished not to be interrupted. Indeed, after a while everyone got used to this.

'Now,' thought Mortimer, 'to escape from marmot land for a short adventure would be good training. Let's have a go!'

Chapter 7

Early Preparations

'How deep does the fence go?' Mortimer asked himself as he walked along the boundary of marmot land. The trouble was that the far end of marmot land was sandwiched between the main road outside the zoo, called Outer Circle, and the aquarium. The fence along the roadside was embedded in concrete, but everywhere else it had been dug into the ground.

'I could dig down under cover of those bushes,' he mused as he made his way over to a large clump. 'Yes, this would be a good place to start.' Mortimer regularly seemed to talk to himself in this way; it helped him to think out loud.

First, he looked around to make sure no one had seen him. With the coast clear, he darted into cover. There was plenty of room for him to move about under the bushes and spread the soil from his digging. After all, this was a secret adventure and he must not leave any clues about. At one point the bushes actually came right up against the fence. He was very excited and started to dig. The soil was soft, and in no time the

35

hole was quite deep. Just as quickly he realised he could not get the soil out if he dug straight down.

'Silly me,' he scolded himself. 'Plan this thing properly. Dig at an angle.' So he started again and found this worked. He was spreading the earth about when someone shouted.

'Hey, you, what are you doing in there? Come out at once!' said the voice.

Mortimer froze. Had he been caught already? What should he do? The voice shouted again, more urgently this time, but Mortimer was unable to move or make a sound because he was so terrified. The voice shouted several more times and then said 'What kept you so long? Come on, we must hurry or we'll miss the bus.' It was a father calling to his child.

Mortimer could relax now so he sat down. He felt a little funny in his tummy after that. On the one hand he had had a terrible fright, and on the other he was relieved to know he had not been caught. After a short rest Mortimer went back to his digging. His first tunnel, two feet down, struck the fence. He tried again another foot deeper, but with the same result. This happened twice more before he found the bottom of the fence.

He was exhausted shovelling the soil out, so tired in fact that he slipped and fell down to the bottom of the shaft, part of which collapsed on his back. He had been careless and had done nothing to make sure that the sides were safe from falling in. He lay still for a while to rest and get his strength back. He wiggled his toes and tail; they were working all right. He tried to lift his tummy off the shaft floor but was stuck tight. It

was getting hot down there and breathing was becoming difficult. He tried again, but could not move. Panic began to grip him. Fear welled up inside him and without thinking he drew back his hands, stuck them into the soil, took a deep breath and pushed backwards with all his strength.

Nothing happened; he was stuck tight. He tried the same thing again, in total panic this time. Push, push, push! He began to move backwards just a tiny bit. He drew an enormously deep breath and tried again. A little more movement was possible but the further back he went the more his chin was pressed down. Breathing was almost impossible now and he could not avoid sniffing some soil up his nose, which to make matters worse made him sneeze. A sudden enormous sneeze gave him a final backward thrust before he fainted from exhaustion. When he came to, he felt quite light-headed, but he was not trapped any more. Even so, he was not a happy marmot just now and wanted only to go home.

He clambered very, very carefully out of the hole so that no more earth fell in from the sides and looked about to make sure he was safe before limping home on his sore feet and stiff muscles. He had had a very close shave with danger. Then, just as he was about to go into his burrow entrance, his father called out.

'Mortimer, what on earth have you been doing?'

Mortimer jumped limply with fright, for he was very tired. 'Hello, Father,' he replied weakly. 'How are you?' he asked, hoping to dodge his father's question, and avoid coming out into the open. Sadly, he did not succeed because his father came right up to him – close.

'You're filthy, boy,' commented his father. 'You've been digging. Why? Burrow not good enough? Trying to escape?' His father's questions were actually meant as more of a joke, but Mortimer was terrified because he did not realise that.

'I thought it would be nice to have a weekend burrow all to myself,' he said without thinking, his voice a little wobbly.

'A likely story!' said Otto. 'Clean yourself up – and fast! Your mother wants to see you.' With that Otto turned on his tail and disappeared. Mortimer slipped quickly into his burrow for safety, relieved that his father had gone but worried about what his mother wanted him for.

As he cleaned himself up, Mortimer thought about what had just happened and wondered if he needed help on his adventure. He thought about confiding in his brother Albert, but Albert was rather talkative and one never knew whether he would be able to keep such a secret really secret. Mortimer decided that it would be best if he did everything himself. Pity, because he liked his brother very much; he was good fun.

Looking terribly smart, Mortimer went off to see his mother. Luckily there had been nothing for him to worry about as all she wanted to do was to measure how tall he was for the family records as he still seemed to be growing.

During the next two days, Mortimer went back to his hole by the fence and excavated a chamber on the far side of it. Unfortunately, he had hit problems with rocks as he dug upwards on the other side, which made the work very dangerous. Then it rained and flooded the tunnel. This meant he had to re-engineer the main entrance to provide better weather protection.

When near the top of the hole he scraped out a hollow to catch water in case it rained before finally breaking through to the other side. He poked his nose through the grass, sniffed to make sure it was all clear, and looked out. It was almost dark. Suddenly, a very bright light shone straight at him. He froze with his eyes tight shut and waited to be grabbed – he was too tired to drop down into the tunnel. An engine started up and the light moved away – leaving him in total darkness.

Chapter 8

Reconnaissance

Mortimer pushed his nose out of the tunnel and through the grass, sniffed the air and listened carefully. It was a dark and noisy night, perfect for him to try out his escape tunnels and look around the zoo and test his plans before he made his real escape. He eased his body out and darted through the shadows towards the gate. The roar of London's traffic reminded him to keep his guard. He stood still by a traffic bollard just inside the gate and watched two cleaners walk straight towards him. He shut his eyes and wished they would go away. They did. Then he scurried across to the African aviary, disturbing the parrots and making them squawk and shriek, creating an awful din.

Mortimer was a bit frightened now. He could not go back that way. He scanned the horizon, saw the restaurant and took refuge amongst the rubbish bins. Immediate danger struck again as a worker nearly trod on him. Unseen, he hoped, he darted to the end of the building and stopped. The danger passed just as he spotted a huge tunnel under the road. Excitedly, he ran through it and leapt into some bushes on the other side. His heart was pounding.

'Will I find my way back?' he asked himself. 'I must be brave.' He breathed slowly and deeply to gain confidence. Calm once more, he set off to find the canal. He was disappointed to find that the sides were very steep, too steep for him to think about sliding down into the water and swimming his way out of the zoo. Continuing his reconnaissance, he passed the llama and camel pens. The cattle and horses came next. Suddenly there was a terrifying noise. It was an enormous moose sounding the alarm – it had never seen a marmot before!

THUMP, thump went Mortimer's little heart as he leant against the fence to calm down again. He had to keep alert. Looking around, he was surprised to see marmot land on the other side of the road. Curiously, he realised that he was really enjoying himself now. He turned on his heel and walked to the bridge over the canal and wandered along past all the pheasants, owls and other birds until he came to the east bridge by the tunnel. Bravely, he strutted through to the shop, scampered across to a tree and hid in the dark as his eyes scanned the night. To his left were pelicans and flamingoes, each standing on one leg while they slept, and to his front was a pond with a fountain in the middle of it.

To get home, he decided to follow a path past the knobbly-kneed flamingos. Unknown to Mortimer, he was not the only animal on the loose in the zoo that night, and he was quite unprepared for what happened next. A deep growl filled Mortimer with

fear. He inched his way forward until he saw the lions and tigers – behind bars! He relaxed a little and sniffed the air. All was well again, he hoped, though a particular scent bothered him. Then again he heard the same deep growl, more menacing this time. Horror, what horror as Mortimer realised that the smell and the growl belonged to each other in the shape of an enormous guard dog on the loose.

For a moment Mortimer froze. He had to do something. The dog charged at him. He turned and ran blindly into the night. They both hit the bars of the rhino and elephant cage at the same time. Mortimer crashed through the bars and as he fell he could hear the yelps of pain from the dog. Almost instantly Mortimer was unconscious as he knocked himself out again.

Sniff, sniff, sniff noises Mortimer began to hear. He was waking up, his heart racing from his fright. Hot breath wafted over his face. He dared not move. Was this the dog sniffing at him, he wondered. Then a soft, tickly thing with whiskers sniffed his face again. He could just make out the thing and followed it up to a face. It was an elephant. Mortimer felt he had turned to jelly and he twitched with fear. Luckily for him, the elephant soon lost interest and moved silently away. But where was that dog, Mortimer wondered?

For some time he dared not move. Everything was very quiet, and when he felt brave enough he drew himself up to look around. There was no sign of the dog. That made him feel better. He moved slowly and searched carefully for some way of climbing out of his problem. A log leaning against the top of the wall gave him his escape route. He climbed up it very, very slowly and quietly so as not to disturb anything. Then, back on the path, he shot off past the storks and stopped at the reptile cage to make sure all was safe. Through the noise of the night he could hear heavy breathing and choking noises. These signalled serious danger again, and deep growls and barking reinforced his fear.

Mortimer had no time to think – he dashed blindly for all he was worth to marmot land. Bang, crash, wallop. The dog had got him. He felt the dog's hot nose and breath on his scalp as it started to close its jaw. With a scream and a flurry of his fists, Mortimer pushed himself away. Then his world went round and round as he tumbled over and over and down and down. He seemed to be falling forever and winded himself as he landed at the bottom of something. Somewhere he could hear frantic growling, barking and digging. Dirt splattered into Mortimer's eyes and he turned his head to get away before realising he was safe. Oh what luck, he had landed in one of his escape tunnels!

'Whoopee!' he shouted out loud, and then crawled back into marmot land. As he came out of his tunnel he noticed spiders' web gossamer threads glinting with dew in the moonlight. The leaves of the bushes glistened as though after rain.

'What a beautiful world,' he whispered to himself. 'I'm safe. But what an adventure! That really was exciting!'

Mortimer had grown up a lot that night. So much

had happened that he wondered whether he really was brave enough to carry out his objective. Back in his burrow he was asleep before he could think of any answer.

Chapter 9

Disaster

The next day, Mortimer felt a shiver go up and down his spine when he looked at the damage the dog had done to his tunnel exit. He hid in the bushes and watched as a keeper filled in the hole. Inquisitive as ever, Mortimer went down to investigate the damage. He felt quite safe now and was not in the least suspicious when he found a ball of white putty-like stuff at the bottom of the outside shaft. He sniffed the ball and liked the smell. He rolled it around and picked it up for another sniff. It seemed good enough to eat, so he took a bite, but as he sank his teeth into it a cold chill suddenly came over him. Something seemed to tell him to spit it out at once. He did, even though it tasted rather nice.

Later that afternoon Mortimer began to feel unwell. His belly felt funny, sort of fluttery, and then worse as it began to hurt. He was sick and running a temperature. He settled himself down on his bed to ease the pain, but it got worse and worse causing him to pull his knees up to his belly. He also had a raging thirst.

47

'What is the matter with you?' his mother asked when she saw him. Mortimer could hardly speak. His mother was horrified as she watched him writhing about in pain.

'Water, water,' he gasped. 'Please get me some water.'

'No,' said his mother. 'If you are this sick you must not eat or drink for at least a whole day. Lie there. I will look after you.' She scuttled off to tell the family and fetch a flannel to cool his face and comfort him.

Morning came after a terrible night. Mortimer was worsening by the hour. His stomach pains caused him to cry out loud and his raging thirst and thundering headache made him think he was probably going to die. Otto and Birgitte did not know what to do. What could they do? They had never seen anything like this before.

'Get the vet,' Birgitte ordered, remembering there were such people. Otto disappeared to tell Mr Beard, meanwhile Mortimer's brothers and sisters dragged him as carefully as they could out into the sunshine for examination.

'It's rat poison,' said the vet, 'quite definitely rat poison. But how did he get it?' Mortimer was too ill to tell him and Mr Beard was quite unaware of the dramas at the end of Mortimer's reconnaissance out of marmot land. He asked questions of the staff.

'It must have been me,' said a guard. 'Yesterday I found a hole by the wire. It seemed like a rat hole which one of the guard dogs had started to dig at. I put some rat poison down and filled the hole.'

'Oh,' said Mr Beard, 'so the little rascal tried to escape after all. Will he die?'

'Hard to say,' said the vet, 'it depends on how much he swallowed and how long ago he did it.'

Everyone was terribly worried. The vet rushed Mortimer to his surgery, placed him in a cat box and gave orders that Mortimer was not to be disturbed except by the nurse who would give him foul-tasting medicine and take his temperature every so often. For three days and nights Mortimer's life was slipping ever nearer death.

Chapter 10

The Great Escape

The twilight world of a cat box in a vet's surgery struck Mortimer as an awful place to die, let alone get better. Slowly he began to feel less pain and to take an interest in life again. It had been a close-run thing. Two weeks later the vet let Mortimer go home, providing he took things easy. After two days back at his burrow, well tended by his mother, he started to feel bored and told his mother so.

'A bored person has an empty mind,' she chided him. 'There are lots of things you can get on and do, so get on and do them. No ifs, buts or maybes. Action, my lad.' With that his mother left him to his own devices.

'All right,' he called after her, then added in a whisper: 'I'll escape!'

Mortimer had a remarkable memory. He knew the map of London as well as any taxi driver. He also knew all the roads in the South-East of England and those through France, Germany and Austria as well as any long-distance lorry driver. Walking his way to Austria was clearly out of the question. This convinced him that he would have to use vehicle transport. But how was the problem he had to solve. He dared not approach a human and ask for a lift, because if he did he reasoned that on the one hand he might be taken back to the zoo, and on the other he could not guarantee that anyone he spoke to was actually going his way. However, he was definite about escaping by night.

Mortimer had lost a lot of weight during his illness. His mother set about fattening him up again, and before long he was fighting fit. Forging ahead with his escape plans, Mortimer thought it sensible to take some rations with him. He collected mini Mars Bars and other things from the zoo shop on 'little outings', as he called them. On one of his hunting trips he found a very small bag with some sweets in it. He converted it into a knapsack and it bulged with his gatherings. He was ready.

'The moment has come,' he said to himself, shivering and tingling with excitement. 'I am ready to go now.' It was just past midsummer's day and the evenings were starting to shorten slightly. 'I wonder how long it will take. I might not get there by winter or get there at all.'

He looked round his burrow den for the last time, felt a little sad at leaving home, and then set out into the warm sunshine. In his mind he imagined Austria and the mountains that stood through all the year like dark, solid walls, revealing their valleys and mounds in clear autumn air and covered in snow and ice. They seemed to call to him, 'come home, come home'.

Storm clouds gathered, the sun disappeared and

soon it was dark. Mortimer set off for the bushes as thunder and lightning started to bang and flash about him. The hour had come. He went straight to his main tunnel and slid to the bottom. Then fear suddenly struck him. Water was pouring in from the storm. Soon he was up to his middle in mud and was afraid he might drown. He put his head down and swam to the other end of the tunnel as quickly as he could and scrabbled upwards for what seemed ages. He kept slipping as the shaft walls came away in his paws. Suddenly he was out in the rain. A light flashed. A dog growled. What a nightmare this was turning out to be!

Terrified now, he blundered along half-blinded by the rain. He reached the outside fence and pressed his nose against it to see what was on the other side. A crack of thunder deafened him but the flash of lightning lit up a turnstile exit on the way out to Camden Town station. He squeezed under the turnstile but became caught by his knapsack; he was trapped. He struggled and struggled but could not free himself.

Someone came running. Mortimer closed his eyes waiting for capture when suddenly he felt himself spun round and flung out into the road. The running sound disappeared. Cars rushed by and lightning was still flashing around. Mortimer got up quickly and darted to the safety of the bushes along the pavement. On his way he tripped and fell, crashing into a road sign. But he had escaped. He was free. He was out of the zoo. 'Whoopee!' he shouted to himself.

The biggest adventure of his life had now begun. Quickly he made his way along narrow streets bordered by houses, and was glad the rain was washing the mud off him. The traffic was heavy and sometimes car lights dazzled him. Whenever he saw a human he would duck in through a gate and hide until the coast was clear. He did not want to be caught, but it was the dogs he feared most.

Mortimer made his way as far as Varndell Street and was just turning the corner into Hampstead Road by the National Temperance Hospital when something bumped into him. Terrified, he jumped to his right and fell through some railings. He lost his grip and landed ten feet down in a basement. Winded by the fall, he hid behind some dustbins while he collected his thoughts.

Clearly humans were going to be a problem. He could not trust them to help him now, and so it would only be safe to move when they were least likely to be about. He would hide up during the day. But first he had to find a safe haven. He climbed gingerly up some steps and was off again, dodging in and out of gates and doorways. After what seemed a long while he reached Trafalgar Square. He saw the statue of Lord Nelson, the forbidding look of the National Gallery, and the pigeons. Oh, how he wished he could fly!

He was very tired now, and being close to St James's Park threaded his way round Trafalgar Square, across the top of Whitehall and through Admiralty Arch to The Mall. He knew exactly where he was. Yes, there was Buckingham Palace visible in the distance as dawn was breaking. He wondered if the Queen was at home.

Mortimer had just entered some bushes on the edge

of the park when a grey squirrel startled him. Recovering his composure, he had a quick look around. He was opposite Horse Guards' Parade and not far from Downing Street. Here he felt safe, sat down and rubbed his sore paws, noticing that his claws had been worn down a bit. Then he dug himself a small chamber, curled up and went to sleep.

Mortimer woke with a start. It was late afternoon and there was quite a commotion outside his temporary lodgings. Creeping forward, he looked out to see all sorts of faces looking in at him. 'Hello,' he said in a friendly sort of way, but they all fled – squirrels, ducks and a lady blackbird. Something scrabbled out of his knapsack; it was a mouse. 'Cheeky thing,' thought Mortimer as he took out a partially nibbled mini Mars Bar.

As it was probably too dangerous to leave the shelter of the bushes just then, Mortimer waited patiently until dusk. Then he set off again, down through Downing Street avoiding the policemen outside No. 10 where the Prime Minister lived, and into Whitehall. Scurrying along to the Houses of Parliament all was going well until a deafening noise knocked him off balance. It was Big Ben chiming ten o'clock. A little numb now, he struggled past Waterloo Station and on until he reached the Old Kent Road. There, surrounded by piles of rubbish bins, he rested to calm down before setting off for Blackheath, where he stopped to sleep for the day.

That evening, when things had become quiet, he carried on his way, darting through the traffic until he reached the main road to Dover at Bexley. The parallel roads of a dual carriageway confused him a bit, but he muddled his way along until he came to a very large Rover garage. He stopped and looked at the huge car transporter parked there, filling up with fuel. Here was a chance he could not miss. He charged across the road, just, only just, avoiding being run over.

Taking cover beside a fuel pump, his heart pounding as if in his mouth, he could hear two men talking.

'Yep, I'm taking this lot to Paris,' said one. Mortimer could hardly believe his luck. The lorry reversed away from the pumps and stopped by some cars.

'Help me lower the ramp and put the cars on, will you?' asked the driver.

'Yes, okay. Lower the ramps,' was the reply. The cars were loaded. Mortimer took a deep breath and rushed over to the lorry and hid behind a wheel. Once the cars had been tied down, he moved to the back. Safely out of sight, he tried to jump up and just managed to hook a claw onto something, but he could not pull himself up and fell down on his back. He tried several times and still with no luck. Then a man came round the back of the truck. Mortimer stood absolutely frozen still, terrified.

'Yeah, the lights are all working okay,' the man said.

Mortimer was at his wits' end now. What was he to do? He made one last huge effort, and without realising it he managed to jump high enough and haul himself up onto the ramp of the lorry just as it started to move off. It jerked horribly and Mortimer nearly fell off, but managed to cling on to a tie-down hoop on the floor. The lorry then stopped. Mortimer seized his chance and ran under a car and grabbed a strut in the steering mechanism. The lorry moved off again and Mortimer held on tight until he could find a safe place to perch. He felt terribly excited.

'Austria here I come!' he shouted at the top of his voice to no one in particular. Suddenly the lorry braked very hard, an emergency brake with squealing wheels. Mortimer was thrown forward, lost his grip and fell.

Chapter 11

Dover and Beyond

When Mortimer fell he landed on the ramp and rolled up against a car tyre. He had been knocked out and when he came to he heard the screeching of brakes as the lorry slowed down on its approach to Dover docks. The lorry stopped two or three times for the driver to speak to someone. Finally, the lorry climbed a hill and went down the other side where it stopped and the driver jumped out of the cab, slammed the door, walked round the lorry and said, 'Good, everything seems to be okay.' He then walked off somewhere.

Mortimer felt safe to come out of his hiding place. He dropped onto the ramp below, from where he could see amber and white lights everywhere, and most exciting of all, the ferries. He edged along for a better view of the port area and was amazed by the number of lorries and cars waiting to go. In the grey mist of dawn he could see the white cliffs above the town.

He was thirsty and, spotting a puddle not far away, tried to find a place on the lorry low enough to jump

59

off. Eventually he reached a wheel arch, which looked like a good ladder. He slipped down to the ground, checked all was safe, and crept over to the puddle. The water was cool and he had a long drink. Just as he was wiping his whiskers things suddenly started happening. He heard new noises, vehicles starting up and beginning to move. Before he knew it, Mortimer's lorry started to move; he rushed back to get underneath it so that he could jump back on to it somehow.

The lorry stopped. Mortimer lunged for a wheel and started climbing up. The lorry moved, and he fell onto his right shoulder, but managed to roll out of the way just before the wheel squashed him. He managed to duck back under the lorry. Quick thinking was called for. It seemed that all he could do was to hide under the lorry and move forward with it until it finally came to rest on the oily deck of the ferry. As the lorry mounted the ramp, a bright torch was shone underneath catching Mortimer in its beam for an instant. A guard dog barked and strained at its leash. Mortimer felt terrified. Then the lorry stopped.

'Come here,' growled the dog handler as the lorry moved forward. Mortimer had to act quickly and was able to jump up high enough to grab a brake pipe. Swinging like a monkey, he held on for grim death as the lorry moved on. Then it did what seemed to be an emergency stop. Mortimer lost his grip and fell, but luck was still with him. He was under his own lorry and the guard and his dog were nowhere to be seen.

'Hi, Tom,' someone yelled over the noise. 'What's that under your lorry?'

Mortimer had rolled into a ball and lay still. Through a half open eye he could see his driver's feet moving round until clear of the back wheels. The driver looked under and stared. Mortimer suddenly felt both sad and very annoyed that he should be caught having got so far on his journey. How could he explain who he was and what he was trying to do? For a moment, his world stopped.

'Some dirty old cloth, I think,' the driver reported. Mortimer held his breath.

'Never,' said the other man. 'I'm sure it was an animal of some kind. Have another look.' Mortimer sprang quick as a flash to hide behind a wheel on the same side as his driver.

'Funny, it's gone now. Perhaps it was the ship's cat,' replied the driver as he went off to join his friend.

Mortimer hardly dared breathe a sigh of relief and his heart was pounding fit to bust. He had escaped detection. He stayed still, frozen in his determination not to be found. Soon he heard a deep rumbling sound beneath him and became aware that the ferry was moving. He now felt safe enough to have a crafty peek about under his lorry. The deck was deserted so he climbed back aboard to find a suitable hiding place in a car engine compartment. Having found one, he settled down for some food and a nap.

The ferry slowing down woke him up. He eased himself out of his temporary bed and hid behind one of the tie-down shackles. He had to be very careful as it was very noisy and people were moving about. Something suddenly gripped and shook his tail. His eyes almost popped out of his head with astonishment. Just as quickly his tail was free – it was the driver checking all the tie-down straps. 'Phew, that was close,' Mortimer said to himself. The ferry came to a stop, the lorry started up and soon they were in France. He knew he was in France because the air smelt different. Mortimer could hardly believe his luck that his escape had gone so well so far.

The lorry drove off slowly over some terrible bumps and through some barriers and soon they were on their way. It was a lovely day with not a cloud in the sky. Mortimer thought Calais a pretty ugly place, what with rows and rows of factory buildings, and oil and gas terminals belching foul-smelling stuff up tall, shiny chimneys into the atmosphere.

After leaving Calais, Mortimer had some thinking to do. His lorry was going to Paris. The lorry was on autoroute E17 to Rheims and at some point it would join the E15 to Paris. Mortimer needed to stay on the E17. He had to get off somewhere. How could he do it? If he could not get off at the junction he could wait until Paris. He knew enough of the map to then make his way, but it would add greatly to the time it would take to get to the Alps.

The sun was shining and the day was nice and warm. Mortimer could have basked in the sun all day as it was so nice on his fur. But no; he had to get off, so he started making his way to the right-hand edge of the lorry because that was the side nearest the grass verge, as Continental drivers drive on the right-hand side of the road and not the left as the British do. It was not easy to move because the lorry was snaking along the road and going terribly fast. He had to use

his claws to grip whatever he could until he reached the side and could cling onto a shackle. The wind rushed through his hair; it was a lovely feeling of freedom. Soon he realised he had to decide how he was going to get off the lorry before it took him all the way to Paris. He did not have long to make up his mind because almost immediately a sign appeared at the edge of the road indicating the E15/E17 split only one kilometre ahead. The lorry was whizzing along, very fast still. At this point he made his way smartly to the back of the lorry. He had to look down. It was terrifying, but he knew he had to jump off or end up in Paris. But jumping off at this speed could easily kill him. He had to take a chance. He summoned up his courage, took a deep breath, closed his eyes, rolled himself into a ball and tumbled over the side. Hitting the ground with a deathly thud, he was aware of a rushing wind, terrible pain, not being able to breathe and then darkness.

Chapter 12

Disaster and Recapture

The sun hung full and clear and bright in the midst of the blue sky, awakening all the smells from heaven and earth, which rise far above the land. The bees were flying to the flowers they sought and the birds were singing cheerily in the bushes and trees. Rooks cartwheeled in the sky and a large buzzard sat on a fence-post beside the road looking for prey in the grass verge. In such a place the traffic rushed by unaware of the dramas, the excitements and the tragedies that lay close by. One of these was Mortimer. He was very alone. He closed his eyes again and tried to forget the pain. It seemed the buzzard had not spotted him – yet.

Mortimer must have drifted off into sleep because when next he opened his eyes he could see only stars in a very black sky. The pain in his body welled up as he remembered falling off the back of the lorry and landing on the side of the road. The base of his tail and his right back leg had taken the brunt of the fall, and he imagined that he must have rolled for some distance down a bank before coming to a stop in the bottom of a ditch made of concrete slabs.

The pain was intense and getting worse. His head ached, his shoulders ached and his back was indescribably sore. He tried to move, but no part of his body would respond. He was paralysed in his panic, quite unable to concentrate, especially as the world seemed to be spinning around in front of him. He slipped back into unconsciousness. When he next woke up he thought for a moment that he was dead. But no, he was alive. He knew he was because it was light again and he could recognise where he was and hear the wonderful sounds of the early morning birds' chorus with them starting up their singing one by one until it reached a crescendo of sound. The rooks were making their usual cawing racket – what a noise, even over the sound of the traffic rushing by. He looked to see if the buzzard was still there – it wasn't; perhaps it had seen a mouse to eat and had flown on somewhere else. His pain seemed to have eased a little so he tried to move. He could just lift his left arm and foot and tilt his head slightly. He tried to roll over but could not stand the pain. Perhaps some things were broken.

'Be patient,' he imagined he could hear his mother saying.

He was very hungry and thirsty and he knew it was going to be a long hot day. After a lot of concentration and effort, but with great difficulty, he managed to move enough to get a hand into his knapsack and find a mini Mars Bar. Oh, how he enjoyed it. Later the sky clouded over and it began to get cool. Then rain started to fall and fill the drain. Mortimer was getting very wet and was frightened that he might drown. So with a terrific effort helped by clenching his teeth, he managed to heave himself clear onto some grass. He was exhausted and the pain was even worse. He took several deep breaths and imagined very hard that the pain was going away. It was then that he noticed he could not move his right leg and feared it was broken.

Through the day and the next night Mortimer drifted in and out of consciousness. Just as dawn was breaking on what must have been the third day he heard the sounds of a car braking and stopping close by. Doors opened and excited voices could be heard, followed by the sound of hissing water. What was happening? The language seemed strange. Then Mortimer realised it was German for 'I'm bursting for a wee!'

'Hey, Dad, come over here and look at this,' a young voice said.

'Look at what?' came the reply.

'It's a marmot,' the child shouted. Mortimer was aware of humans gathering around him and groaned, 'Help me, please.'

'You're right,' said the father, 'and it looks as if it's been badly hurt. Really, who would do such a thing to a defenceless creature like this? Fetch a blanket.'

Soon the groaning Mortimer was being lifted tenderly into the back of the car.

'I think my leg is broken,' Mortimer murmured quietly.

'Did you hear that, Dad?' said Peter, the boy.

'Hear what?' asked father.

'I'm sure I heard the marmot say "I think my leg is broken". He did, I'm sure of it.'

'Impossible,' said the father, 'animals can't talk!'

'Yes, I can,' squeaked Mortimer, 'and my leg is broken.'

'Goodness me,' said the father, 'he can talk! What an amazing animal. What's your name?'

'Mortimer.'

'Mortimer, Mortimer,' said the father. 'You are badly hurt and very wet. We will take care of you.'

You can imagine the excitement of the family at this discovery. First of all an injured marmot, and wonder of wonders it could talk – in German too! The children were beside themselves with excitement and wanting to help.

'Be careful,' ordered the mother as Mortimer was lifted up and laid down on a soft rug in the back of the car to be dried off very gently with a white towel.

'Yes, your leg is very badly injured,' said the father. 'We must get you to a vet or you will die.' Mortimer groaned and let out a sob.

'But, Helmut,' said the mother, 'we are already very late and we have to get home fast for your meeting with the mayor tonight.'

'Yes, Helga,' came the reply. 'I know. I tell you what though. This is a very special animal. We will take him home and call out our vet there – if he lives that long. He would make a lovely pet.'

'No,' said Peter. 'Please take him to a vet now. He might die if we don't.'

'Peter,' said father. 'We have to go straight home now. You know that. We will get the vet as quickly as we can. I will call him on the mobile.'

Mortimer, despite his pain, was very happy now

because he realised he would probably be well cared for, especially if they wanted to keep him as a pet. Not only that but he would probably also be closer to his destination. Nobody talked for some time, and the children were really very unhappy that Mortimer had not been taken to a vet. Meanwhile Mortimer lay reasonably comfortably on the blanket in the back of the car. He liked having his head stroked by the children. Peter had two sisters, Sophia and Anke, and they took turns in comforting Mortimer. The journey seemed awfully long, but Mortimer did not seem to mind as this family would take care of him. He really perked up when he heard the word 'Worgl' mentioned. He became very excited now because Worgl was a small town in Austria and a landmark on his route to the Hoch Gletcher.

It was late evening when they arrived home. The vet arrived just as the family had placed Mortimer in a basket in the kitchen. The vet lifted the groaning Mortimer onto the kitchen table and started to probe about. Mortimer shot into the air when his right leg was touched and he let out a very loud screech, 'OOOOOUCH!' but he did not speak as he was not sure he liked this vet very much because he seemed a bit brusque, not like his vet in London.

'His leg is broken,' said the vet, 'but the rest of him seems all right apart from some pretty heavy bruising. I'll make a splint and bandage his leg. I've got to go to Innsbruck tomorrow. Would you like me to take him to the zoo?'

'No, no!' shouted the children. 'Dad, you said we

69

might be able to keep him,' they chorused. Mortimer gurgled with delight.

'Children,' father spoke sternly, 'this is a wild animal and it could be dangerous.' Father did not say anything about Mortimer being able to speak.

'No, no,' said the vet very quickly, 'this one is quite tame. He's been somebody's pet.' Mortimer could only just stifle a little chuckle – if only they knew the truth. He would tell them one day.

'Well, whoever it was obviously got fed up with him and slung him out on the autoroute,' opined Helmut. 'Do you really think he should go to the zoo?'

'No, don't let him go. Please, please may we keep him?' the children pleaded.

Mortimer was beginning to feel a little faint with pain now and really did not mind where he went as long as he could get well again. The vet sorted out the broken leg and settled Mortimer down into the basket. He could be given food and water and lots of comfort.

'I tell you what, children,' said their father a little more kindly, 'together with the vet we will look after him until he gets better and then decide what to do.'

'Hurray, hurray!' they shouted and danced around the room in glee. Mortimer was content because whatever happened, once he was better he could attempt to escape and continue his journey. He was very cooperative and kept very quiet until the vet had gone. Then he fell asleep as the children stroked his head.

And so Mortimer was carefully looked after for a number of days and told the family about his time at

London Zoo, and also about his plans. They wanted to know why he ended up where they had found him. He was not worried about them knowing as he knew he could escape quite easily if he really wanted to. The vet called daily, but never knew that Mortimer could talk. The family kept that a very strict secret just to themselves. All the family friends who came to visit were very kind to this little furry friend. Mortimer really liked Peter and Sophia, who spent lots of time telling him secrets about their school and friends. They had long conversations together. Anke was too young to go to school, but she loved Mortimer and often tried to lift him up – but he was almost too heavy for her. She would whisper into his ear make-believe stories about her toys. Mortimer loved it and would lie there patiently listening very intently.

Because of their fascinating way of life in the wild, and their general behaviour, marmots have long been kept in captivity. Even so, Mortimer was not really keen to settle down as a pet, though he enjoyed all the love and attention he was given, because he still had his objective of reaching the Hoch Gletcher before winter set in. So reluctantly he decided to plot his escape.

While plotting, Mortimer behaved himself well. He was allowed to move freely about the house and was sociable with everyone he met. He became very popular with the children's friends. After a while his leg was fully mended, his bruises had gone and he felt fit enough to escape. He gradually started changing his behaviour. He stopped nuzzling the children and became distinctly less friendly to everybody. If a stranger approached he would shake and beat his tail back and forth, gnash his teeth, stand erect and lunge at the stranger and try to bite. The children were sad and puzzled by Mortimer's changing behaviour, especially Anke, but even so they still loved him. They guessed he wanted to escape and continue his adventure.

Soon, though, the parents resented the naughtiness and realised that Mortimer was clearly a young marmot who was growing up into adulthood. It was difficult for the children to understand that animals, no matter how tame they are, when they grow up want their freedom – especially if they are meant to be wild animals in the first place. Some of the things Mortimer did were very naughty. For example, he climbed on the furniture and nibbled it; he bit buttons off cushions and clothes and turned over the coal bucket every time it was filled. He collected socks, shirts and other garments with which to line his living basket, and tore at towels hanging on the bathroom rail until they fell. He started eating house-plants and gnawing at closed doors. He tried all sorts of ways of escaping but was thwarted every time. He decided that for his tactics to work he must stop speaking to anyone. If he was to be sent to the zoo before he could escape from the house, he would have to delay his escape until then.

'That's enough,' said Helmut one day. 'He doesn't talk to us any more and has become really quite wild. He's got to go. We will take him to Innsbruck Zoo this very afternoon.' The children cried and were frustrated because they would rather Mortimer escaped. Anke thought it would have solved all problems if they just opened the door and bade him goodbye. With a twinkle in her eye, Anke began to think. She loved Mortimer dearly and wanted so much for him to be happy. She would help him.

Chapter 13

Innsbruck Zoo?

So, to the zoo it was to be. Mortimer wondered what the zoo would be like. He had heard about it from Mr Beard in London. Mortimer was furious to be taken to the zoo in any event and would only let Peter or Anke handle him now. This upset Sophia. It was with a very heavy heart that Peter picked up Mortimer and put him into a carry-box, which he put on the back seat of the car between him and Anke.

Peter started crying as the children got into the car, and he couldn't understand why Anke was winking at him. In fact, he was sure she was even smiling! Smiling? How could she smile when they were having to take Mortimer to the zoo and give him away into captivity where he would never get away?

'Thank you very much,' Peter imagined the keeper would say in a very kindly way to Peter as he held Mortimer tightly in his arms before handing him over. 'We will take great care of him and you must come and visit him often, children.' Peter gave a big sniff and reached for his handkerchief as he thought about the sadness he was about to experience. He bit his lip as he tried to be brave when the car started to move. Sophia noticed this and tried to reassure Peter that Mortimer would be well cared for.

'The zoo is famous for its marmots and they have a lovely time,' said Sophia, who had been reading up about it. 'The marmots used to live more outside their cages than in them. They would bite the wire and dig tunnels under the walls of their outdoor cages and run in and out. The keepers were quite happy except when the marmots were a nuisance to pet dogs, which roamed around the place from time to time. Male marmots,' she said seriously, 'have a habit of rushing at a dog and trying to hang onto its neck by their teeth. All this was fine and dandy until a new fox compound was built next door to the marmot pen. Special arrangements had to be made for its fences because the keepers were worried that the marmots are inquisitive creatures. If Mortimer is anything to go by, they are very inquisitive little creatures. They would dig their way through to join the foxes and the result would be either dead marmots or dead foxes or both.'

'How did you know about all that?' asked Helmut.

'I read about it in that natural history book you gave me for Christmas,' Sophia replied. 'Also, whenever a new marmot arrives the others nuzzle its snout in welcome, because they are desperate to find out who the new marmot is and where he has come from. He might even know some of their relatives.'

Mortimer listened to this and wondered if he would find his new environment interesting and his new friends acceptable. However, he would not be content to stay there. Being a canny creature, he would lead the other marmots into thinking he was happy to be at Innsbruck, especially with them.

It was difficult to turn round in the box and the heater was on in the car. This was not surprising as summer had given way to autumn now and the coolness of the mountain air. Mortimer had noticed that his fur was starting to grow thick to prepare him for the cold winter ahead. He knew that the squirrels were gathering their beechnuts and acorns. The flocks of migrant birds heading south were becoming rarer, and all those creatures which hibernate were preparing for their long winter's sleep. He had noticed that each day the arc of the sun's track from the distant mountains across the sky drooped down more and more. The sun no longer rose so high. It had given life to every living creature and to all growing things, but now was coming the time for them all to be tested by winter's dangers, enemies and unknown trials. Sadly, the weak would die and only the strong would survive through the coming time of hardship. Soon, the snowflakes would fall.

Mortimer wondered whether he would have to wait until next spring before trying to escape again and complete his quest. But no, deep down inside him he felt an irresistible urge to press on as soon as he could. He would have to take stock of the situation and work out new plans. He had lost his knapsack when he jumped off the lorry but was sure he could find sufficient food once he had escaped again, even as he climbed up the mountains and went above the height

77

where no trees grow, where there would be only heather, mosses, lichen and wild berries.

'Not far now,' said Helmut. 'The zoo is just over there.' Peter and Sophia leaned forward to see out of the windscreen. Meanwhile Anke undid the catch on the carry-box. The car stopped suddenly to avoid the one in front, which had suddenly stopped when the traffic lights at the zoo entrance turned red. As everybody was watching the car in front, Anke quickly opened the box, heaved Mortimer out, opened the car door and slipped him out onto the road.

Mortimer hit the road hard, scuttled quickly round to the back of the car and rushed across the road and into some bushes. There he stopped, turned and looked at the car. He could see Anke smiling and waving at him. A lump came into his throat as he stood up on his hind legs, waved a paw and dashed off through some more bushes, which led away from the zoo towards some very tall and dark woods. He didn't have time to think. He was free again, thanks to Anke. She had been a real friend and he was sad that he would never see her again, and that she would get into terrible trouble for letting him go.

Chapter 14

Destination Hoch Gletcher

Immediately after he had escaped, Mortimer scuttled towards the woods. He flattened himself on the ground as a car sped by causing whirling air to ruffle his thickening fur. Quickly, up and away, he rushed across a street and made good his escape into the countryside. Frost was forming and, apart from the sound of cars in the distance, the night was suddenly quiet, dead quiet. Wisps of smoke rose lazily from the rooftops of houses and stars twinkled in the moonless heaven above him. Mortimer was pleased with the way things were going. It was getting late as he made his way south from the city to climb up over some steeply rising open ground with fields lined with fir trees. He found a convenient tree and dug a nest for the night before foraging for his evening meal.

First light came and with it the dawn chorus of birds started. The sky was dark, dark blue and down in the valley a mist was lying over everything like a soft woolly blanket. Mortimer watched in wonder as large birds wheeled about the morning sky. How he wished he could fly! The sun came up and burnt the mist away so that he could now see the River Inn and the E60 autobahn motorway disappearing to the east. Following this road, he would reach Worgl, where his rescuers lived and where he would branch off for Brixen-im-Thaler and Kitzbuhel.

He set off on his way and promptly slipped on some loose pebbles. Laughing at almost landing on his tail, he regained his balance and carried on. It took him several days to reach Kitzbuhel. He had lost count of how many had passed because he journeyed when he could, slept when he had to and fed as often as he liked. He marvelled at the grandeur of the mountains and was very excited by being in the middle of them. He carried on up past Jochberg to Pass Thurn, then down the steep sides of the mountains into the Mittersill Valley.

'Not far to go now,' he said comfortingly to himself.

In the valley he travelled east to Zell-am-See where the road to the Hoch Gletcher started. He followed the river as it was safer than the road where he might be run over by a car or shot by a hunter. The climb quickly became very steep and difficult. Mortimer began feeling very tired and desperately wanted an extra long sleep. But would this be wise? It was fast reaching hibernation time and he dare not really relax for a long snooze for fear that he might wake to find it was springtime. Anyway, he did not have a suitable nest to snuggle into if he was to survive the long winter.

He dragged himself into a niche between two boulders and settled down on the moss. It was bitterly cold and hunger prevented sleep. A furious storm swept in from the north. The wind howled and the snow drove itself into his outer fur. Mortimer shivered. The light was poor and all he could see was barren wasteland, a few trees and rocks. Hunger finally drove him out into the snow to forage for something to eat. He found a fir cone but it had no seeds in it; others were empty too. He stumbled and fell down a small cliff and landed on another pile of fir cones.

'Food, glorious food!' he shouted out above the noise of the storm as he noticed plenty of seeds. He ate quickly, then searched for shelter but there was too much snow, so he rolled himself into a ball with his back to the wind and tried to keep warm as the snow covered him completely. Soon he was fast asleep.

The sun's weak but warming rays woke him. He was terribly drowsy and had to fight hard to wake up properly. The storm had stopped and the trees stood still and icy hard, as though turned to stone. Mortimer felt very alone and rather sad. He really should have found himself a burrow to survive the winter in and avoid any other sort of danger. But, no, he was still being driven on by his determination to reach the Hoch Gletcher.

'On, on, I must go on!' he shouted to the mountains. By now he had to follow the snow-covered road as it was too steep any other way. At one point he stopped in the quiet of the hills and turned round. There in the snow were the most extraordinary marks. He had never seen their like before. Was he being followed? He spun round and round but still could not see anything untoward. Then he realised he was looking at his own footprints. What a goof he felt.

He headed on up the very winding and twisting road past the Edelweiss-spitze until he reached Hochtor. There was little sign of human life apart from one or two mountain huts close by what he recognised as ski-tows, but there were no skiers about. At Hochtor the road had disappeared under the snow and he realised to his dismay that he was lost.

'Don't panic, don't panic,' he instructed himself. 'Just remember the map. REMEMBER THE MAP,' he spoke sternly to himself. He set his face to the wind and sniffed out the north-west. 'The road must be along there,' he muttered and trudged off.

Impatient to continue, it was soon night and the stars twinkled like jewels in the heavens and the moon was just starting to rise, full in its awesome beauty. Excitement gripped him even though he was tired. At one point he stopped for breath and looked back, surprised to find that he was now above the tree line. He was in proper marmot land now, but where were the marmots?

At about midnight, the weather changed quickly, forcing Mortimer to take refuge in a nearby hut full of straw. Deep, deep darkness enclosed him and he could see nothing in the hut, but there were many very interesting smells. If he stood on his back legs and sniffed upwards there was a smell of uncommon sweetness, probably hay, whereas on the floor the smell was sour and covered in muck. Mortimer was trapped there for two days while the blizzard raged.

Continuing on, his heart seemed to jump into his mouth when he saw a very large building that looked like a hotel and restaurant. He recognised it from

Fodor's book about Austria. It definitely was the hotel.

'This must be it,' he cried out happily. 'I've reached the Hoch Gletcher.' He was so thrilled to be where he felt he really belonged. The blizzard had stopped, the sky had cleared to reveal a deep blue and the day was beautiful and sunny, the bright light glinting on the snow-covered ground. He scouted around looking for marmots before he realised that at this height and coldness, marmots were hibernating already. This meant they were all underground in their burrows, safe from the ravages of winter.

Mortimer was worried now as he trudged on through the thick snow up towards the top of the glacier. He spied another little hut in the distance and decided to make for it. A few steps further and he slipped and tumbled into a hole when the snow gave way. He was not hurt, only winded, but decided to rest a while.

'This is a curious place,' he thought. It smelt musty and a little dank. He realised he was in a marmot-made burrow. He went to the entrance and looked out. What he saw was just like a picture in a book he had read. Far below was the Hoch Gletcher and high above was the Grossglockner alp.

'I'm home,' he whispered to himself excitedly. 'I'm home where I belong.' He set about exploring the burrow in the hope he would find some other marmots in there hibernating. But because the burrow did not smell fresh he soon realised that it had been abandoned. However, there was some old bedding and the remains of food in the main chamber.

84

Exhausted after the hardship of his travels, he sat down and stuffed himself with some of the food and then promptly fell asleep.

Months passed by without Mortimer noticing as he dreamed and twitched his way through his first proper winter hibernation. Then the light began brightening earlier in the day over the mountains and fading away later. The days were lengthening but the sun was still weak. Its light flooded the cold, crisp air and the earth gleamed and glittered with white frost. It was still not warm, but green was coming back to the mountains. Mortimer stirred in his nest. He woke up slowly, had a very, very long stretch, yawned and sat up.

'That's funny,' he said to himself, 'Look at me! I'm positively skinny. Gosh, I must have been hibernating. So, if I've woken up now it must be springtime outside. Hurrah, hurrah!' he shouted and hurried to the burrow entrance. He poked his nose out and almost died of fright.

'Who are you?' asked a deep voice.

'I'm Mortimer,' he replied, feeling terrified, to the very old marmot sitting outside looking in at him.

'And who are you?' Mortimer stammered.

'My name is Oscar,' said the old marmot.

'Oscar?' Mortimer suddenly did not know what to do. He was rooted to the spot by a surge of excitement making him feel quite wobbly in his tummy. 'Do you have a son called Otto?' he then managed to ask slowly.

'I did,' growled the old marmot, 'but he disappeared a long time ago with his wife, the day

85

they got married actually, and no one has seen or heard of them since.' The old marmot looked very sad, but Mortimer could hardly contain himself with the sudden excitement of this meeting.

'Otto is my father,' said Mortimer, 'so you must be my grandfather.' Mortimer was stunned by the excitement of it all. 'Hello, Grandpa. I've come a very long way to find you. Oh, I am so excited I don't know what to say,' as he rushed forward to give his grandfather a big hug. The old marmot nearly fell over with surprise.

'How do you know I am your grandfather?' the old marmot asked, hoping and wondering. 'I'd better come into your burrow and you can tell me.'

Mortimer was so excited he fell over and tumbled into the main chamber. Laughing with happiness, he grabbed some food and took a nibble, for he was very hungry.

'Calm down, young man,' said the old marmot. 'Come, sit down here and tell me about it. Oh, pass me a root to eat, I'm hungry too.'

So Mortimer started his story. A long while later, once the old marmot had realised he *was* Grandfather, he insisted that they both go off there and then to meet the rest of the family and tell them the great news.

So Mortimer had reached his objective – HOME! After his long hibernation, he naturally felt a little stiff as he followed his grandfather out of the burrow. The old marmot stopped at the entrance, sniffed the air for danger, then poked his nose out a little further for another sniff. 'Do not forget that eagles are also very hungry in early springtime, and a marmot makes a very good meal for an eagle,' he warned his grandson, thinking he probably did not know about that sort of danger.

Just as he was about to go outside, Grandfather spotted a large black eagle circling over the top of the Gross Glockner alp, but it was far enough away if they made their next move quickly. He crawled out further, stood upright and spun round like a top to make sure everything else was safe.

'Come on, Mortimer, follow me,' said Grandfather with a whistle as he raced up over the top of a rocky outcrop. 'Run fast! Keep close,' he kept shouting as he scampered along a flat grassy bit, then down into a big dip and up the other side. Mortimer lost his footing on a moss-covered rock and had to have another run at it.

'Come on, Mortimer! What's keeping you?' shouted Grandfather.

Mortimer was still feeling a little weak and stopped for a moment to catch his breath. Suddenly, he caught out of the corner of his eye the sight of the black eagle starting to swoop. Where was Grandfather? He had lost him. He was terrified.

'Grandfather! Grandfather!' yelled Mortimer, 'where are you?'

'Here, here, over here, you silly boy,' called Grandfather from not very far away. Mortimer, in blind panic, rushed over to join him. Grandfather was now standing upright outside the entrance to a large burrow.

'Good,' said Grandfather. 'This is our front door.

But before we go in, let's just tease the eagle.' So they stood there waving their paws in the air. The eagle was diving fast with its wings tucked in for speed. Mortimer felt very frightened but dared not show it. All at once he seemed to see two huge bright yellow eyes piercing through him, and two enormous grappling hook-like feet with sharp talons and a large open beak coming straight for his face. He screamed in absolute terror, and as he did so Grandfather pushed him into the burrow.

'Good fun, eh?' asked Grandfather as he scampered in.

'No,' said Mortimer very honestly. 'I've never had that sort of experience before, despite the dangers of my journey here. That was very frightening,' he had to admit.

'Goodness me, Mortimer, we get it nearly every day here. Anyway, that's enough of that. Let's go and meet the family. They will be so excited, especially your grandmother.'

And so, they crawled down the tunnel. Grandfather stopped just inside the chamber.

'Hello, everybody,' he said. 'I have something very exciting to tell you.' There was much muttering and wondering what Grandfather was going to say. 'You will remember many years ago Otto and Birgitte disappeared after their wedding.' There was a chorus of 'Yes'. 'Well, this morning I found out what happened.'

'Do tell us,' the family pleaded.

'It seems that Otto and Birgitte were captured by some kind humans who took them to a place far away

88

and over a very big river. There they were well looked after and had a family. Their eldest, a boy called Mortimer, decided that he would run away and try and find his real home in these mountains.' There was dead silence as Grandfather paused in his story-telling.

'Mortimer, after a very long and dangerous journey, eventually found his way here,' Grandfather continued.

'How do you know?' asked Grandmother.

'Because,' Grandfather continued, 'I found him in our last year's burrow this very morning and here he is!'

At this point Grandfather stood aside and led Mortimer in. Mortimer was a little overcome with shyness as the family gathered round and his grandmother hugged him. After lots more hugs and kisses from uncles and aunts and cousins they all sat down demanding to hear all of the story of what had happened.

So, a long time later, when Mortimer had finished telling his story, the family sat silent. It was Grandmother who spoke first.

'Mortimer, it is so lovely to see you. I miss my Otto awfully wherever he's living now, but this is where we live and call home. Home is where your family is,' she said. Mortimer felt a lump come into his throat and his tummy felt a bit queasy again. 'Your family lives in another place,' she continued.

'I know,' he said quietly, 'and I miss them.' At which point he burst into tears and thought for a moment that his wonderful journey had not been so wonderful after all.

'Would you like to stay here a while and then go home?' asked his Grandmother.

'Yes,' Mortimer replied quietly through his tears.

'That's good,' said Grandfather. 'We will give you the best holiday you could ever have. We will introduce you to all your relatives and our friends. We will tell you all about our lives here and show you all our favourite haunts.'

'Yes, yes,' said an uncle, 'and then let us all take Mortimer home!' There was much cheering. Mortimer sat silently for a moment, wiping a tear from his eye.

'That sounds like a lovely idea,' said Grandmother. 'I would like that. It would be wonderful to see Otto and Birgitte again and to meet the rest of my grandchildren.'

'Yes,' said Mortimer, smiling happily again. 'But right now, I'm very, very hungry! Please may I have something to eat, Grandma?'

The end ... for now!